MY INDEX 0 : AN OFFICE LOVE STORY

HARSHI

Made with ♥ on the Notion Press Platform
www.notionpress.com

Contents

Title Verso

Title: " My Index Zero: An Office Love Story"
Author: Harshi
Published by: Self-published.
Publishers Address: Tenali, Guntur dist , Andhra Pradesh, INDIA.
Printer : Published Online on various platforms.
ISBN : 978-93-341-3329-5

Author's Note

Hello Readers,

In this book, I have included some ABAP theory topics that are italicized. Feel free to read them if you're interested in learning more about ABAP, which is the profession of Tarun (the male lead). Otherwise, you can skip the italicized content and continue with the story.

CHAPTER I

Tarun

Best Tech Solutions, B City

The first hour in the office was quite chaotic as everyone was busy preparing for the morning meeting. As a new employee, I felt a mix of nervousness and excitement. I had joined the company as a team lead, bringing with me two years of experience.

Almost everyone was already in the meeting room when a woman walked in. She immediately caught my attention with her charismatic appearance and well-defined body shape. What truly captivated me were her delicate collarbones, drawing my gaze whenever I could steal a chance. Despite being in the company for a week, I hadn't encountered her earlier. She introduced herself as Swastika, Senior Team Manager, who would lead our team for the current project.

Initially, I expected her to be strict and unapproachable given her bold looks and serious expression. However, as the meeting commenced, she turned out to be quite friendly.

Three hours later, when the meeting finally ended, I let out a sigh of relief and stepped out for a stretch. However, soon enough, I realized I had forgotten my notebook inside. As I returned to retrieve it, I found Swastika in the room, gathering her belongings.

Approaching her, I noticed her eyeing my notebook with interest.

"What's this?" she inquired, flipping through the pages.

"Just some notes I took during the meeting," I replied, feeling a twinge of embarrassment as she examined my work.

Swastika simply laughed and handed the notebook back to me.

"You have a neat handwriting," she remarked with a grin.

Blushing at the compliment, I thanked her before quickly exiting the room. Though I couldn't shake off the feeling of having made a fool of myself, I couldn't deny the excitement bubbling within me at the thought of getting to know Swastika better.

Over the next few days, as we worked together, I found myself drawn to Swastika's sense of humor, often laughing at her witty comments. Despite our friendly conversations, I still felt somewhat intimidated by her. There was an aura about Swastika that made her seem superior to everyone else as if she had experienced things beyond our understanding. Her mysterious persona intrigued me, and I wanted to learn more about her.

One evening, lost in my thoughts, I unconsciously found myself walking towards Swastika's desk.

Just as I realized my mistake and turned to retreat, Swastika noticed me and asked, "Do you need my help with anything?"

My mind scrambled to come up with an excuse. "Um... I was thinking... maybe we should create zviews for the project. Since the client is requesting data from different tables."

Swastika nodded in agreement. "Yes, that could be a good approach. Review the document and come up with potential solutions before our next meeting. We can discuss it with the client then."

I nodded feeling relieved. “Okay, I’ll do that.”

As Swastika began to wrap for the day, she asked, “Is there anything else you need my help with?”

“No,” I replied quickly, grateful for the chance to escape further scrutiny.

With that, Swastika left, and I let out a sigh of relief.

*

The Next Day

After working continuously for some hours, our team decided to take a quick break. I took this chance to make small talk with Swastika.

“Hey, so I heard you refer to your boss as ‘Loop’. That’s an interesting nickname, how did you come up with it?”

One of the things that amused me about Swastika was her use of SAP ABAP terminology as nicknames for the people around her. I found it hilarious and couldn’t help but laugh every time she used them.

“Oh yeah, ‘Loop’. Well, he tends to repeat things over and over again during meetings, so it just stuck.”

“I can imagine how that can be annoying, but I guess it makes for a funny nickname. Do you have any other nicknames for your coworkers?”

“Hmm, let me think. There’s one guy I call ‘Conditions’ because he always sets specific conditions for everything we do.”

I laughed. “That’s clever. I bet he loves that nickname.”

“Yeah, he’s not too thrilled about it, but he knows I mean it in good fun.”

“I like that you can have a sense of humor at work. It makes the days go by easier.”

“Definitely. Plus, it helps to have a good working environment.”

"I think I have a perfect nickname for Steve," I said, excited to contribute to her list of nicknames.

"Oh yeah? What's that?"

"I think we should call him 'Switch'. He's always changing his mind and flip-flopping on his decisions."

She chuckled. "I love it. That's a perfect nickname for him. I'm definitely going to start using that one."

"It's a fun way to bond with our colleagues and make work a little more enjoyable."

"Agreed. I'm looking forward to coming up with more nicknames for the rest of the team."

*

Once, I decided to ask Swastika about her life outside of work.

"So, Swastika, what do you like to do in your free time?" I asked, trying to keep my tone casual.

She looked at me for a moment. "Well, I like to read and watch movies. I also enjoy traveling when I get the chance."

I nodded. "That's cool. What's your favorite book or movie?"

She smiled. "I love 'Ikigai: The Japanese Secret to a Long and Happy Life' and the movie 'Inception'."

"Good choices. Have you traveled anywhere interesting?"

Swastika's smile faltered slightly. "Not really. I've only been to a few places, nothing too exciting."

I could sense that there was more to the story, but I didn't want to push too hard.

That evening, even after I left the office, I couldn't stop thinking about her. I kept wondering why was she reluctant to talk about herself. It was as if she was hiding something. I was determined to find out more about her and help her in any way I could.

As I walked towards my car, I decided to take the opportunity to ask her out. “Hey, Swastika, do you want to grab a drink sometime?”

Swastika looked at me with a smile. “Sure. That sounds like a good idea. When were you thinking?”

“How about the Friday night?”

“Friday works for me,” she replied, her eyes twinkling with excitement.

As we exchanged numbers, I couldn’t help but feel a sense of elation. I was finally going on a date with the woman I had been admiring from afar for so long. But, I also knew that there was a lot more to Swastika than met the eye. I was determined to uncover her secrets.

As we said our goodbyes, I made a mental note to do some digging before our date so I wouldn’t make any mistakes that would upset her.

CHAPTER II

Tarun

Brew Bar

I took a sip of my wine and cleared my throat.

"Is everything okay?" I asked, breaking the awkward silence.

She looked up at me. "Yeah, I'm fine. Just thinking about work, I guess."

I nodded, understanding the feeling. "Work can be stressful. I've had my fair share of tough days." I chuckled.

She smiled back at me, but it didn't quite reach her eyes. "Yeah, I know. You always seem to handle it so well though."

I shrugged. "I just try to keep a positive attitude and take things one step at a time."

She nodded, her gaze still distant.

Noticing her worry, I decided to ask her about it. "You know, Swastika, I can tell that there's a lot more to you than you let on. I want to know more about you and your life."

She looked at me with a sad smile and said, "There are things that I've been through that I don't like to talk about."

I immediately regretted bringing up this topic. Changing the subject, I asked, "So, have you thought of any other nickname for our colleague, Switch?"

Her eyes lit up, and she laughed. "Oh, I've been thinking about it all day. How about 'Flip-Flop'?"

I grinned. "I like it. It definitely fits."

The conversation continued, and I was happy to see her mood lighten up a bit.

As we left the bar that night, I couldn't help but think about her sad smile. Maybe she didn't trust me enough to share her secrets? Or maybe I was just not close enough for her to share her secrets?

I kept thinking about it all the way home. I would have hit someone with my bike if it wasn't for the late hour and low traffic.

I felt defeated. I had tried to get closer to her, but I only pushed her away. I knew that I had to be patient and wait for the right moment to try again.

*

Over the next few weeks, Swastika and I continued to work together, but there was tension between us.

But, one day, as we were returning from a meeting, Swastika suddenly turned to me with a mischievous smile. "You know, Tarun, I've been thinking about your nickname. I think I have a good one for you. From now on, I'm going to call you 'Code'."

I looked at Swastika, puzzled. "Why 'Code'?"

She laughed. "Well, it's simple. You're always coding, and you're the best at it. So, why not have a nickname that reflects your talent?"

"I guess that makes sense. I like it. From now on, I'm Code."

As we continued walking, she started teasing me with the new nickname. "Hey, Code, can you code a program that can make me coffee?"

I couldn't help but laugh. "Maybe someday," I replied. "But if you want it immediately, you can ask your Code. He can make it for you."

From then on, everyone in our team started calling me 'Code'. It felt strange at first, but I quickly got used to it. I started introducing myself as 'Code' in our internal team meetings and conferences.

*

A few days later, at another meeting, Swastika approached me again. “Hey, Code, I have another idea for you. Why don’t you start a coding blog? You can share your knowledge with others and help them improve their skills.”

I was taken aback. I had never considered starting a blog before.

And so, I started my coding blog, sharing my knowledge and experience with the world. I received a lot of positive feedback and comments.

All of this started with a simple nickname. I was grateful to Swastika for coming up with it. It not only reflected my talent but also gave me the confidence to share my knowledge with others.

She often gave me valuable feedback to improve my blogs and writing style.

One day, I asked her, “Hey, Swastika, have you checked out my latest blog post?”

“Not yet. But, I’ll definitely give it a read later. You always have great tips and tricks for coding.”

I laughed. “You give me too much credit.”

“No, seriously. You’re one of the best coders I know. And now, everyone in the coding community knows it too, thanks to your blog.”

“I couldn’t have done it without you. You gave me the confidence to start sharing my knowledge.”

“That’s what friends are for. And, who knows, maybe someday you’ll be teaching coding classes or writing books on the subject.”

“Let’s not get ahead of ourselves. But, who knows; anything is possible.”

"That's the spirit. Keep coding and keep sharing your knowledge. The world needs more coders like you."

CHAPTER III

Tarun

Best Tech Solutions, B City

The office was buzzing, as usual, and everyone was engrossed in their tasks. I was deep in my work when I heard a clapping sound. I looked up to see Swastika standing at the entrance of the room, her face lit up with excitement.

"Hello, everyone!" she called out, her voice brimming with energy. "I have an announcement to make."

"There's a coding competition coming up in our city soon," she continued, her smile wide. "It's a big deal. Companies from all over the country will be there, showing off their best talent. And, guess what? We're going to be a part of it too."

I nodded along with everyone else, intrigued but assuming this was just a general announcement. That was until Swastika's eyes found mine. She pointed directly at me and grinned, and my heart dropped just a little.

"And, I'm thrilled to announce that Tarun will be representing our company!"

As every head in the room turned toward me. I sat back in my chair, half stunned, half flustered.

"What? Me? No, no, I'm not sure if I can do this," I blurted out, shaking my head. This was way out of my comfort zone. I loved coding, but I wasn't sure about stepping into the limelight.

Swastika walked over to me, and the look in her eyes was one I'd seen many times before — full of faith, full of confidence.

"Tarun, you're the best coder we have. You've handled every project that has come your way with skill and creativity. This is your chance to show everyone what you're capable of."

The rest of the team chimed in, their encouragement flooding the room.

"You've got this, Tarun!"

"Come on, Tarun, you're the guy for the job!"

"We're all behind you!"

I could feel the walls of doubt crumbling a little, especially with Swastika standing there, looking at me like she knew I could do this. And maybe, just maybe, I could. I rubbed the back of my neck, still feeling the weight of their expectations but also the warmth of their support.

Finally, I sighed and managed to pass a smile. "Alright, alright, I'll do it. I'll represent our company."

The room erupted into cheers. "That's the spirit! We're all here to support you every step of the way."

As the excitement settled and everyone went back to work, I sat there for a moment, processing everything. This wasn't just a coding competition anymore — it was a chance to represent, not just myself but my entire team, my company, and especially Swastika, who had always believed in me even when I doubted myself.

With Swastika managing the preparations and keeping me on track, I knew I wasn't going into this alone. She was right there, my biggest supporter, guiding me through the whirlwind of practice and planning.

The road ahead wouldn't be easy, but with Swastika's unwavering support, I was not afraid.

*

The CG Hall

On the day of the competition.

The bustling conference hall was alive with excitement as participants from all over the country gathered for the highly anticipated coding competition. I walked in with Swastika by my side, soaking in the vibrant atmosphere filled with tech enthusiasts, programmers, and industry experts.

"Are you ready for this?" she asked, giving me a supportive smile.

I nodded confidently, feeling the familiar rush of adrenaline. "More than ever. This is going to be fun."

I glanced around, taking in the sight of the other competitors, most of whom were huddled around their screens, making last-minute tweaks to their code.

Swastika was my biggest supporter and the one who had been with me through every step of this journey. She'd organized everything meticulously, from our registration to ensuring I was mentally prepared for each round. We made our way to our designated spot, and I set up my laptop, mentally running through the stages of the competition: the debugging round, the algorithm challenges, and finally, building a functional application using ABAP.

"Remember, you're one of the best here. Just keep your focus," Swastika whispered, leaning over.

I smiled at her, grateful for her unwavering confidence. "Thanks, Swastika. I couldn't do this without you."

A loud beep echoed through the hall, signaling the start of the first round. I dove into my screen, eyes scanning lines of code, searching for bugs that had been deliberately planted. My fingers moved swiftly over the keyboard as I began to identify and correct the errors.

Here's some background on ABAP debugging:

ABAP Debugging Theory:

In ABAP (Advanced Business Application Programming), debugging is a crucial skill that helps developers identify and resolve issues in their programs. The ABAP Debugger allows developers to run through a program line-by-line, inspect variables, evaluate expressions, and determine the flow of logic.

Key debugging techniques include:

Setting Breakpoints: Temporary markers that pause the execution at a specific line of code. These can be either static or dynamic.

Watchpoints: Conditions set on variables that pause the program when the variable reaches a specified value.

Step Into, Step Over, and Step Out: Commands used to control the flow of code execution, allowing developers to dive deeper into functions or skip over certain lines.

I finished the first round with time to spare, and when the scores came out, I was among the top.

I stretched my arms and looked over at Swastika, who gave me a thumbs-up. “Great job! That was smooth.”

The tension in the room ramped up as we moved into the second round, which involved algorithmic challenges. This was my comfort zone, but I knew I needed to stay calm and not rush through it. I worked methodically, crafting solutions that were both efficient and elegant.

ABAP Algorithmic Theory:

In ABAP, algorithms are constructed using basic control flow statements and advanced operations to manipulate data effectively. Key concepts include:

1. <u>Control Flow Statements:</u>

- IF, ELSEIF, and ELSE: Used to implement conditional logic, allowing for different code execution paths based on

varying conditions.

- CASE Statements: Useful for evaluating a single expression against multiple conditions, simplifying the decision-making process.

- LOOPs: Various forms like `DO`, `WHILE`, and `LOOP AT` are employed to iterate over internal tables or execute repetitive tasks until a certain condition is met.

- EXIT, CONTINUE, and CHECK: Manage loop control, such as breaking out of loops, skipping iterations, or validating conditions before processing further.

2. Data Processing Techniques:

- Sorting: Organizing data efficiently with `SORT` statements to prepare for faster searches and comparisons.

- Searching: Utilizing `READ TABLE` or `LOOP AT` statements to locate specific entries in internal tables.

- Aggregating: Combining values using `COLLECT` or summation loops to consolidate data.

3. Optimization Techniques:

- Nested Loops: Although sometimes necessary, nested loops should be minimized as they can significantly impact performance.

- Binary Search: With sorted tables, employing `READ TABLE ... BINARY SEARCH` reduces search time from linear to logarithmic complexity, enhancing performance.

4. Recursion and Iteration:

- ABAP supports recursive methods, allowing problems to be broken down into sub-problems. Recursion is useful in tasks like traversing hierarchical data, but care must be taken to avoid stack overflow due to deep recursion levels.

These algorithmic principles help build code that is not just functional but also optimized for speed and resource utilization.

After finishing the second round, I was a bit winded but satisfied.

I looked at Swastika and said, "This one was tricky, but I think I nailed it."

"You did amazing," she said, handing me a bottle of water. "One more to go."

"Yes, the final round."

CHAPTER IV

Tarun

The CG Hall

The final round was the big one — building a functional application using ABAP. I knew this was where I could shine. I'd spent countless hours honing my skills for this moment.

The timer started, and I threw myself into the work, fingers flying across the keyboard, translating lines of code into a working application. I could feel Swastika's eyes on me, watching every keystroke as I brought my vision to life.

ABAP Application Development Theory:

ABAP applications typically consist of various concepts such as Reports, Module Pool Programs, Function Modules, and Classes. An end-to-end application may include:

Database Layer: Data storage and retrieval using Open SQL statements like SELECT, INSERT, UPDATE, and DELETE.

Presentation Layer: Creating interactive screens using ALV Reports (ABAP List Viewer), or designing user interfaces with Dynpros (Dynamic Programs).

Business Logic Layer: Implementing core business logic in Class Methods, Function Modules, or Subroutines.

Key Concepts Tarun Implemented:

Selection Screens: Takes input to filter records for displaying.

Internal table: For data processing. Structures that store data temporary.

ALV Reports: For presenting data in an interactive and user-friendly manner.(output)

I was lost in my element, focused solely on my screen.

As the clock ticked down, I ran a final test, making sure everything worked flawlessly.

"Time's up!" the host announced, and the room went still.

I took a deep breath, feeling the weight of the competition lift.

Swastika turned to me, beaming. "You were incredible. I've never seen you so focused."

I smiled back at her, feeling the relief wash over me.

As we waited for the results, the judges meticulously reviewed each application, testing functionality, and efficiency.

It was finally time for the results. Everyone was nervous.

When they announced the winner, I couldn't believe my ears when they called my name. I was so happy; I was on cloud nine.

"Congratulations! I knew you could do it!" Swastika exclaimed, her eyes sparkling with pride.

I went on stage, and the judges presented me with the trophy.

The next day, after office hours, our company organized a success party for me in a private room at a cosy restaurant. The atmosphere was filled with laughter, music, and a sense of celebration. As soon as I walked in, everyone turned to me with cheers and applause. My colleagues congratulated me one by one, patting my back and raising their glasses in my honor.

The party was lively, with people mingling, sharing stories, and indulging in delicious food and drinks. I could see Swastika in the crowd, chatting happily with some of our team members, her face glowing with pride. She caught my eye and gave me a wink, raising her glass in a silent toast. I smiled back, grateful for all the support she had given me.

Drinks flowed freely, and everyone seemed to be in high spirits, enjoying the evening to the fullest. The music played in the background, setting the perfect mood as we all let loose and celebrated the victory. It was one of those moments where the stress of work melted away, replaced by the joy of being surrounded by friends and colleagues who had been a part of the journey.

As the night went on, we laughed, clinked glasses, and shared stories of the competition. I couldn't help but feel grateful for the incredible team that stood behind me, pushing me to do my best. This celebration was not just about my success — it was about the collective effort, the late nights, and the unwavering support that had brought us all here.

Everyone drank to their hearts' content, enjoying the night without a care in the world.

CHAPTER V

Tarun

A Few Days Later

On the Street

As I was returning home as usual after clocking out, I saw a group of men trying to tackle someone. It seemed like they were trying to force that person inside a car.

I was stunned. I had to act fast. I didn't know who the person was, but I couldn't just stand there and watch.

As I got closer, I realized that it was Swastika. She was struggling, but the attackers were too strong.

I quickly jumped in, throwing punches and kicks as fast as I could. I wasn't sure if I could take them all down, but I had to try. I focused on Swastika and made sure to keep her safe from harm.

After a few intense minutes, the attackers stepped away. I felt relieved but also exhilarated. I couldn't believe what had just happened.

Before I could talk to Swastika, I noticed some people emerge from the shadows, but she signaled them to stop. They went back into the shadows, not wanting to be noticed.

Thinking I didn't notice that, she started behaving like any normal girl would do in this situation.

"Thank you so much for saving me," she said, her voice shaking slightly.

I could tell that she was not as frightened as she tried to show me.

"I had to. I couldn't just stand there and do nothing," I replied.

"I don't know how to repay you. You put yourself in harm's way to save me."

"Don't worry about it. I'm just glad you're safe."

"No, really. I owe you one. How about dinner? Let me treat you to a nice meal to say thank you."

I was very excited. Trying to maintain my composure, I said, "Sure, that sounds great. I'd love to have dinner with you."

As we walked away from the scene, I couldn't help but feel like I had just saved the most important person in the world.

I was nervous as we arrived at the five-star restaurant, wondering what our date was going to be like.

We ordered drinks and started to chat about our day at work, slowly easing into the conversation. As we talked, I realized how much I enjoyed Swastika's company. She was smart, funny, and easy to talk to.

The food arrived, and we savored each bite, enjoying the delicious flavors and each other's company. We talked about our hobbies and our dreams for the future. However, I was the one who was talking all the time. She replied occasionally with a line or two to it. Maybe she was a bit distracted by that incident.

After we finished dinner, we bid goodbye to each other.

*

Swastika

Swastika's Home

Lately, I have been getting used to Tarun so much. I like talking with him and spending time with him. I know he has a crush on me. But, I am not sure if I will be able to take another chance at love after what happened in the past.

My phone rang, interrupting my thoughts, and I knew exactly who it was.

"Hello, dear sister. How are you doing?"

"Hello, Brother. I am good. But, enough with the pleasantries. I know you won't call me without any reason. Now say, what is it?"

"Haha! You catch up on everything very quickly."

"I heard that a hero rescued the damsel in distress."

"News sure travels fast. I can't hide anything from you."

"Who is he?"

"He is my colleague. A junior employee at work."

"Oh! Only a junior? Nothing else?"

"No, there is nothing between us."

"Really?"

"Um... Maybe he has some feelings for me. I can see it."

"And, what about you?"

I thought for a moment and answered, "I-I don't have any feelings."

I touched my face; it felt warm. Oh my God! Why the hell was I blushing?

"Oh, really? Then why are you shuttering?"

"Who is shuttering? I did not."

"Ok! Ok! You are not. But, he seems to be a good guy. I should be the first one to know if you guys were to be in a relationship. Ok?"

"Yes, Brother."

My brother was not someone who would easily praise others. This gave me hope to look forward to work tomorrow, so I would get to see Tarun again.

"Let's get serious now. Do you know who tried to kidnap you?"

"Yes! It is them. It is definitely not a coincidence."

"What sh*tty people! Why can't they leave you alone? I think it is high time I taught him and his family a lesson. If we stay quiet, they will think we are some kind of pushovers."

"Okay. This time I won't stop you. Do whatever you have to."

CHAPTER VI

Tarun

Best Tech Solutions, B City

I came to the office early in the morning and sat at my desk, waiting for Swastika. But, I didn't expect her to enter whistling in a low happy tone. Everyone started looking at her in shock as she walked past them.

"Hey, Swastika, you seem to be in a good mood today. What's up?" I asked.

"Oh, nothing much. Just feeling a little playful, I guess."

"Playful? What do you mean?"

"I don't know, I just feel like making some jokes and being a little flirty today."

I was surprised when she said that. "Flirty? You?"

"Yeah, me. Why not?" She giggled.

"I don't know. It's just not something I'm used to seeing from you."

"Maybe you just haven't been paying enough attention," she said leaning in.

She was so close, I felt a little flustered. "What do you mean?"

"Oh, nothing. Just that maybe you've been so focused on work that you haven't noticed some of my other qualities."

"And what other qualities might those be?"

She leaned back and said, "Hmm, I don't know. You'll have to figure that out for yourself."

I felt a little intrigued by her words. "I think I might just do that."

As the days went on, I found myself increasingly drawn to her flirty side. I began to notice her playful comments more often and found myself looking forward to seeing her at work.

*

One day, we had to give a presentation that would decide the future of our project. All the people in the conference room were higher-ups, and I couldn't help but feel a little nervous around them. However, the presentation turned out to be a success and the project started soon.

As we were working on the project together, Swastika leaned over and whispered in my ear, "You know, I think you're really cute when you get all flustered."

I could feel my face turning red, and I tried to hide my embarrassment. I wasn't used to being on the receiving end of Swastika's flirtatiousness, and I didn't know how to respond. But, she just smiled and went back to work, leaving me to wonder about what had just happened.

Later that day, as we were taking a break, I mustered up the courage to ask her, "So, uh, what was that all about earlier?" I asked.

She just grinned and shrugged. "Oh, it is nothing. I just thought you look cute when you're a little flustered. It's kind of adorable, actually."

I felt my face turning red again, but this time I couldn't help but smile. Swastika's playful banter was starting to grow on me, and I found myself enjoying the attention.

"Well, maybe you'll have to try to make me flustered more often."

She laughed and gave me a playful nudge.

"Challenge accepted," she said with a wink.

From that moment on, our work sessions were filled with playful banter and flirty comments. I found myself becoming more and more comfortable with her, and I realized that her attention wasn't something to be intimidated by, but something to enjoy. It was a fun way to pass the time, and I couldn't wait to see what Swastika would say next.

As I sat with Swastika during our break, I couldn't help but admire how beautiful she looked in the sunlight.

Suddenly, she suggested we play a game of pool, and I quickly agreed, hoping to impress her with my skills.

After work, we went to a nearby bar. Her playful and flirtatious mannerisms intensified with every shot she took on the pool table. She was clearly enjoying the game, and I couldn't help but be entranced by her every move. I tried to focus on the game, but my eyes kept wandering back to her.

I found myself growing more and more aroused as we continued to play, and it was becoming increasingly difficult to hide my feelings from her. She seemed to sense the tension between us and was playing it up even more.

"You're pretty good at this game," I said, trying to break the silence.

"Thanks, I've had some practice," she replied with a sultry smile.

I felt my heart rate rise at the sight of her smile.

"I can tell," I said, trying to keep my voice steady.

She leaned in closer to me as she took her next shot.

"You're not too bad yourself," she said, her breath hot on my ear.

I felt a shiver run down my spine at the sensation of her proximity.

"Thanks," I replied, feeling my face flush with desire.

As we continued to play, the sexual tension between us grew stronger, and it was becoming harder to focus on the game. Swastika seemed to be enjoying this dynamic, and I wasn't sure how much longer I could hold out.

As we reached the end of the game, Swastika leaned over and whispered in my ear, "You know, I think we make a pretty good team. Maybe we should work on a project outside of work sometime."

I turned to face her, feeling my heart pounding in my chest. "I'd like that."

She smiled at me, and I could feel my desire growing stronger with every passing second.

I asked, "Are you really ok with this?"

"Yeah, I was thinking that we could do something creative. Maybe work on a design project or something," she replied with a smile.

"Oh, design... Yeah!" I scrambled. I felt stupid as I realized how badly I had misunderstood her intentions. "That sounds amazing," I said, trying to sound calm. "When would you like to start?"

"How about this weekend? We can meet up at a coffee shop and brainstorm some ideas," she suggested.

Earlier, I was not even able to let her have her guard down. But now, things had changed a lot. I grinned, feeling a rush of excitement at the thought of spending more time with her.

"I'm free on Saturday. Let's do it."

As we gathered our things and left the bar, I couldn't help but feel like my life was about to take a thrilling turn.

Just then, she kissed me on the cheek, sending a shiver down my spine.

I knew that this was just the beginning of something special, and I couldn't wait to see where this journey would take us.

CHAPTER VII

Swastika

Swastika's Home

I jolted awake, my heart racing from the nightmare that had haunted my sleep. The memories of that past incident flooded my mind, filling me with fear and uncertainty. I shook my head, trying to push the thoughts aside, as I realized it was time to start getting ready to meet Tarun.

But then, a nagging doubt crept into my mind. What if Tarun turned out to be just like Anirudh and Amod? The thought sent a shiver down my spine, but I quickly dismissed it. No, I couldn't let the actions of a few define my perception of everyone else. Tarun was different. I had to believe that.

Shaking off the lingering doubts, I forced myself to focus on the present. I got out of bed and began to prepare for the day ahead, determined to face whatever challenges lay ahead with courage and resilience.

*

Tarun

Coffee Shop

As we sat down at the coffee shop to brainstorm ideas for our project, I couldn't help but notice a shift in Swastika's demeanor. Her flirtatious behavior seemed to have disappeared entirely, and she appeared more guarded and distant than she had been before.

I decided to break the ice and said, "So, what ideas do you have for our project?"

She paused for a moment before responding, "I was thinking maybe we could work on a photography project."

I was pleasantly surprised by her suggestion. "That sounds great. What kind of photography project were you thinking of?"

She shrugged her shoulders. "I haven't really thought it through. I just know that I love taking pictures, and I thought it would be a good way for us to work together outside of work."

I nodded in agreement, feeling excited about the possibility of collaborating with her. But, as we continued to discuss the details of our project, I couldn't shake off the feeling that there was something on her mind today.

Curiosity got the better of me, and I asked, "Is everything okay? You seem a little different today."

She looked up from her notebook, her expression guarded. "What do you mean?"

"I mean, you're not as cheerful and flirtatious as you have been lately," I said, trying to tread lightly.

She looked down at her notebook, and there was a long pause before she finally spoke. "I'm sorry if I gave you the wrong impression before. I tend to use flirtation as a defense mechanism. It's just my way of keeping people at arm's length."

*

Swastika

"You don't have to keep your guard up with me," he said, his eyes locking with mine. "I want to get to know the real you."

I was taken aback by his vulnerability, his willingness to see beyond the facade I had put up. As he reached out to take my hand, I felt a rush of emotions, a mix of surprise and relief.

For a moment, I hesitated, unsure if I could trust him with my true self. But then, his sincerity broke through my defenses, and I found myself nodding slowly.

From that moment on, our relationship changed. We continued to work on our project, but now there was a new depth to our interactions. As we delved into our creative pursuits, we also delved into each other's lives, sharing our pasts, hopes, and fears. And, with each passing day, I found myself letting go of my fears, allowing myself to be vulnerable in his presence.

His presence brought me a sense of warmth and comfort, a feeling I hadn't experienced in a long time. It was as if he had a way of soothing the wounds of my past, of making me feel safe and cherished. And, as I looked into his eyes, I knew that I was ready to take a chance on love again.

I started opening up to him, and finally, I told him a bit about my past.

*

A Few Months Ago

M City

I met this guy named Anirudh at an art gallery, drawn to his charm and charisma. We hit it off instantly, and soon enough, we were dating. After a whirlwind romance filled with travel and adventure, he proposed to me, and at that moment, I felt like the luckiest person alive. The happiness was palpable, and I was certain that nothing could break us apart.

But, fate had other plans. Anirudh invited me to his house for a surprise, and although I was excited, there was a niggling feeling of doubt in the back of my mind. When we arrived, he proudly declared that he had decorated the house himself, and alarm bells started ringing in my head. Knowing him, he was never the one to bother with the finer details. He always asked his domestic help to arrange everything. So, when he claimed to have decorated the house himself, it seemed out of character, and a small voice in the back of my mind warned me that something was amiss.

When we went into the room, he began kissing me, and immediately, his touch became forceful. I pushed him away, rejecting his advances, but he didn't take no for an answer. His demeanor changed, his eyes darkened with anger, and before I knew it, he had become violent. Panicking, I fought back, managing to land a hit and break free from his grasp. With adrenaline coursing through my veins, I fled from the house, my heart pounding with fear and disbelief at what had just transpired. It was a nightmare I never saw coming, shattering the illusion of love and safety I had once felt.

After I told my brother everything, he did some investigation, and it turned out that Anirudh was arranged by the villainous guy Amod to hurt me. My brother was furious and wanted to take revenge. But, I convinced him to let Amod go for once since he was supported by his family of heinous people.

The whole ordeal had left me feeling shaken, but I knew that I had to be strong and not let anyone take advantage of me again.

Later, my grandfather found out about the incident and decided to send me to B City for my safety. He managed to arrange a position for me in his friend's company and insisted that I relocate. Despite my best efforts to plead with him to reconsider, he was resolute in his decision.

*

Tarun

Best Tech Solutions, B City

I had come to realize that Swastika was a mature and composed person. She was someone who didn't share much about her life, and I was always curious to know more about her. Although we talked about her past in the coffee shop, there were still so many things I didn't know about her. Despite that, we had a good working relationship.

During one of our breaks, I decided to lighten the mood and share some of my embarrassing work moments with her. I told her about the time when I had sent an email to the wrong person, causing chaos in the office. I could feel my face turning red as I recounted the story, but Swastika's laughter was infectious.

"Wow, Tarun, that's quite the blunder." She chuckled. "I can only imagine the look on your face when you realized what you had done."

I couldn't help but laugh along with her. "Yeah, it was pretty bad. But hey, we all make mistakes, right?"

She smiled at me. "You're right. It's important to be able to laugh at ourselves and move on."

CHAPTER VIII

Swastika

Best Tech Solutions, B City

As I listened to Tarun's stories, I couldn't help but laugh along with him. His ability to deal with his embarrassing moments in such a fun way was admirable.

"I can't believe you spilled coffee on your old boss." I chuckled, shaking my head. "I'm sure he appreciated the new shirt though."

He grinned sheepishly. "Yeah, he did. But, it was definitely a hint for me to be more careful around hot beverages."

I smiled at him, feeling grateful for the moment of lightheartedness. "You know, I always admire people who can find humor in tough situations," I admitted. "It's a great quality to have."

Tarun's eyes met mine, and I could see the warmth in them. "Thanks. I've always believed that life is too short to take ourselves too seriously. We have to learn to laugh at ourselves sometimes."

I nodded in agreement, feeling a newfound respect for his outlook on life. "I couldn't agree more."

As we walked back to our desks, I playfully nudged Tarun's shoulder and responded, "Hey, I can be fun too!"

Tarun laughed and said, "I know you can be, and I'm going to make it my mission to bring back your wild side."

I couldn't help but smile at his confidence and determination.

As the weeks went by, he would often come by my desk to tell me a funny story or joke. It was nice to get a break from work and laugh with someone. Sometimes, we would even make up silly nicknames for our co-workers using SAP ABAP terminology, just like how I always did.

One day, as we were leaving the office, Tarun asked me if I wanted to grab dinner with him. I hesitated at first, not sure if it was a work-related invitation or something more. But, he quickly clarified, "Just two friends grabbing dinner. I promise I won't make any more jokes about you needing to loosen up."

I couldn't help but laugh and agree.

*

Ambience Restaurant

Over dinner, he shared more stories about his life outside of work. It was always refreshing to see that warm side of him.

As Tarun spoke, I watched him, slightly taken aback by his confession. "You know, I used to be short-tempered," he said casually as if it was the most natural thing in the world.

"You? I don't think so. You must be joking," I responded, genuinely surprised. It was hard to imagine the calm and composed Tarun I knew as someone with a short fuse.

He chuckled, but there was a hint of nostalgia in his eyes. "It was something that my friends found both amusing and endearing, or so they say, and they often teased me about it."

I listened intently as Tarun recounted his story, describing a night at a local bar with his friends. "One evening, my friends and I were hanging out, catching up and enjoying each other's company. As we chatted and laughed, my short temper began to surface."

"My friends, who know me all too well, just exchanged these knowing looks and grinned," Tarun continued, shaking his head. "One of them tried to keep a straight face but ended up saying, 'Yeah, we heard. You were pretty worked up about it.' They were all trying not to laugh."

I could see Tarun's eyes light up with the memory as he chuckled softly. "I was annoyed, but I couldn't help but laugh at myself. I mean, it's just one of those things, you know? I told them, 'I know, I know. I just can't stand people who drive like idiots.' "

Tarun glanced at me with a sheepish smile. "The funny thing is, as the night went on and we talked about other stuff, my temper cooled off. But then, after a few more drinks, I got annoyed again, this time over something completely stupid."

He paused for a moment, clearly enjoying retelling the story. "I looked at the bill and just started grumbling, 'I can't believe this place charges so much for a beer. It's ridiculous.' My friends just rolled their eyes at me like, 'Here we go again.' They were so used to my temper flaring up over the smallest things."

He finished with a grin, shaking his head at his past self, while I watched him, both amused and intrigued by this glimpse into his old habits.

Hearing all this, I couldn't help but feel amused. It was a side of Tarun I hadn't seen before, and it made me realize how much he had grown. To think that someone who now exuded so much patience and calm had once been quick to anger. It was surprising, but also endearing in its own way. I wondered what had changed him, what had softened those rough edges. Had it been life experiences, or was it the people around him who influenced him for the better?

Towards the end of the meal, Tarun leaned in and said, "I have to admit, I really enjoy spending time with you. You're easy to talk to, and I always have a great time with you."

I smiled, feeling my heart swell with warmth.

"Likewise," I replied. "I'm so grateful to have you as a friend."

"Or more than friends? Maybe?"

I chuckled, and he blushed as usual.

As we finished our meal and headed out of the restaurant, Tarun pulled me into a warm embrace and said, "Let's do this again soon."

I hugged him back, feeling grateful for the way things were going with him so far.

"Definitely." I smiled.

"Can't wait."

*

CHAPTER IX

Tarun

Best Tech Solutions, B City

One day, while working, Swastika looked at me and said, "Hey, are you okay? You seem really upset and stressed."

I sighed. "Yeah, I'm just going through some personal stuff."

"You can talk about it with me. I'm here for you."

I hesitated at first but ended up telling her. "Well, it's mostly financial. I'm struggling to make ends meet and falling behind on my bills. I had a small argument with my father, and he blocked my cards."

She chuckled and then quickly apologized. "Sorry. Is there anything I can do to help?"

I was surprised when she said that. "Oh no, I couldn't ask you to do that."

"Please, I want to help you. Let me lend you some money to get you through this time. You don't have to suffer alone."

"Thank you so much, Swastika. I don't know how to thank you."

"Don't worry about it. I just want to be there for you in any way I can. We're friends, right?"

"Yes, we are. And, I'm so lucky to have you as a friend."

"The feeling is mutual, my friend. Let's get through this together," she said warmly.

Her kindness and willingness to help me in my time of need made me feel like I wasn't alone in my struggles. What if she were to stay beside me for the rest of my life? And, the thought alone filled my heart with happiness.

I felt a weight lifted off my shoulders as I talked to Swastika. I appreciated her understanding and was grateful to have her as a colleague and friend. From that day on, our bond grew stronger, and we became even closer.

While I could easily ask my father for assistance, I couldn't bring myself to swallow my pride and request him to unblock my card.

"I don't think I could have made it through some of these tough days without you."

She smiled back at me, her eyes shining with warmth. "I feel the same way, Tarun. You're always there to make me laugh. And, I know I can always count on you to have my back. I'm glad that we can be there for each other, both in work and in life."

We walked out of the office building together, and I couldn't help but admire Swastika's beauty. She had a simplicity and sensuality about her that was alluring.

"You know, you're not like anyone else I've met before. You're beautiful, and you're also so down to earth," I said, feeling a little bold.

Swastika blushed, "You flatter me, Tarun. But, I think the same can be said about you. You have a sense of humor and warmth that draws people to you."

We continued walking and chatting, enjoying each other's company. I felt so lucky to have Swastika as a colleague and friend. As we parted ways, I felt a sense of happiness and contentment. I knew that no matter what life threw my way, I could count on her to be there for me.

As our friendship grew stronger, I became more and more warm and affectionate towards her. I couldn't help but feel protective of her, and I made it my mission to make sure she always felt safe and comfortable around me.

Days passed by in happiness. But, one day, Swastika was feeling particularly down and vulnerable. I noticed it right away. I decided to enquire about it when we went to the cafeteria for a break.

"Hey, what's going on?" I asked gently, placing a reassuring hand on her arm.

Swastika hesitated for a moment but eventually opened up to me. She told me about the secret she had been carrying around with her. And, as she spoke, tears began to well up in her eyes.

*

Swastika

It all started when I witnessed one of my subordinates in tears, surrounded by concerned colleagues. As I approached to offer comfort, I learned the heartbreaking truth about how a wealthy boy named Amod had deceived her under the guise of friendship and love. His actions had left a trail of broken hearts, with many other victims suffering like her.

The injustice of it all ignited a fire within me, and I couldn't suppress the urge to seek justice for those who had been wronged. My childhood best friend, Arohi, stood by my side, equally outraged by Amod's despicable behavior. We joined forces, determined to unveil the truth, reaching out to other victims in our quest to unravel the patterns and tactics employed by this despicable individual.

That scoundrel Amod seemed to have a penchant for targeting innocent, unsuspecting girls who were new to the city and lacked a privileged background. Such families often kept such incidents under wraps, fearing societal backlash and lacking the resources to confront a powerful family like his.

With this knowledge in hand, we devised a plan. We created a social media profile for me, portraying myself as a middle-class newcomer to the city. Sure enough, Amod took the bait. He engaged in conversations with me, eventually inviting me for lunch. Little did he know, Arohi was discreetly tailing me to the restaurant, ready to intervene if needed.

His plan of action was predictably consistent. He would first lure his victims to a restaurant, gaining their trust before inviting them to his house under the guise of a surprise.

After several outings to various restaurants, the fateful day arrived. This time, when he extended the invitation to his house, claiming to have a surprise planned, I hesitated but agreed in the end. With Arohi by my side, we ensured our team of bodyguards, police officers, and reporters were ready and waiting.

We knew that while Amod's family could easily pressure a few officers, it would be much more challenging to cover up the incident if it made headlines. With everyone ready to spring into action at my signal, we were determined to catch the vile Amod red-handed, ensuring he could not deny his despicable actions.

As I stepped into his house, Amod handed me a glass of mango juice. "Here, have some. It's the only juice I have at home. You don't mind mango, right?"

I hesitated, suspicious of the drink's contents, but he insisted, urging me to take it. The house felt strangely empty, devoid of any signs of the surprise he had promised. I pretended to hold the glass, unwilling to drink, and he noticed.

"Why aren't you drinking? Go ahead, take a sip," he urged, reaching for my hand to force the glass into it. As he pressed the glass against my lips, the juice spilled, drenching me. “Oh no, I’m so sorry. Come, let me help you clean up,” he said, guiding me towards his bedroom.

“Why are we going into the bedroom? Aren’t there separate bathrooms in the house?” I asked nervously.

“This is the only bathroom with a washbasin,” he replied smoothly, leading me further into the room.

Once I had cleaned up my dress, I quickly called Arohi to update her on the situation. Coming out of the bathroom, I found Amod waiting outside and the door locked.

CHAPTER X

Amod

Amod's House

As I waited outside the locked door, frustration gnawed at me. What was taking her so long?

Relief flooded through me as the door finally swung open, revealing Swastika standing there.

Her hesitation only fueled my desire as I approached her with deliberate intent, relishing the tension that crackled in the air. With a grin, I made my move, attempting to draw her into an embrace. I found amusement in her defiance, my grin widening as I pressed on, determined to have my way.

As she struggled against my grasp, I chuckled darkly, enjoying the thrill of the chase.

My patience wore thin as her resistance persisted. Initially, I entertained the idea of savoring my prey, relishing in the fear that danced in her eyes. But, with each passing moment, my desire turned to frustration, and I decided I couldn't afford to waste any more time.

With a swift motion, I pushed her onto the bed, a primal urge driving me to take what I desired. Her cries of fear and desperation only fueled my hunger as I forced myself upon her, ignoring her pleas for mercy. The struggle only served to intensify my hunger, the taste of fear sweet upon my tongue as I reveled in her terror.

"I beg of you, please let me go," she pleaded, attempting to push me away with all her might.

But, I remained unmoved, rooted in place. With a sudden burst of strength, she shoved me forcefully, surprising me with her resilience.

As she tried to flee, her cries for help echoed through the room. "Help! Somebody, please help me!"

I swiftly caught her before she could reach the door, my grip firm as I pulled her back. She struggled in my grasp, her fear palpable as she looked at me with wide eyes, like a frightened animal. Strangely, her panic ignited something within me, a twisted excitement that spread a grin across my face.

"Go ahead, scream," I taunted, egging her on. "Let it all out."

Her expression shifted, confusion clouding her terror as she glanced around the room. I took advantage of her momentary distraction, easily maneuvering her back onto the bed. Tears streamed down her face as she fought against me.

"This room is soundproof, darling," I assured her with a smirk. "Your cries won't reach anyone's ears."

Upon hearing my words about the soundproofing, her complexion drained of color, a look of disbelief washing over her. For a brief moment, her struggles ceased as the realization sunk in. She stared at me, wide-eyed and pale, the fear gripping her momentarily paralyzing her movements. In that moment of vulnerability, I seized the opportunity to assert my control.

With a surge of anticipation, I moved to undress her, unable to contain my eagerness any longer.

*

Swastika

Despite my overwhelming panic and fear, a glimmer of hope flickered within me. I knew there were people just beyond these walls who could rescue me if only I could break free and call out for help. But, his grip was unyielding, crushing any attempts at escape, despite my training in self-defense. I grappled with the realization that, in my current state, I couldn't overcome the physical disparity between us.

Resigned to my circumstances, I devised a different strategy. I feigned submission, biding my time, waiting for the moment when he would inevitably lower his guard. It was my only chance at escape, and I clung to it with desperate determination.

A sense of rationality started to come back into my mind. But, before I could act, he lifted my top, and I paused, ceasing my struggles. Instead, I fixed him with a pained look, biting my lower lip to mask the fear welling up within me. My eyes glistened with unshed tears, a silent plea for him to reconsider. Despite my apparent submission, I made sure to convey my reluctance, hoping to maintain the facade and avoid arousing his suspicion.

His expression spoke volumes as he interpreted my lack of resistance as a green light to proceed. With a satisfied grin, he loosened his grip, inching closer to me as if to claim his prize. Despite my compliance, I instinctively covered my lips with my hands as he leaned in for a kiss.

His hands, once firmly restraining mine, now exerted a different kind of pressure, skillfully pressing against my waist.

"Ahh!" A soft moan escaped my lips as I felt his touch, a mix of discomfort and feigned pleasure intertwining within me.

Seizing the moment of opportunity, I broke free from his grasp and swiftly slipped off the bed, a mischievous glint in my eye as I playfully evaded his advances. With a wink, I taunted him, inviting him to chase after me in a playful game of cat and mouse.

As I darted around the bed, teasing him with each step, I halted near the door, leaning against it with a coy smile. Oblivious to my actions, he trailed behind me, lost in the fervor of his pursuit.

In a daring move, I allowed him to draw closer, his kisses grazing my cheek, jawline, and neck. His focus consumed by his lust. He failed to notice my hand sneaking towards the lock.

With a deft maneuver, I quietly unlocked the door and darted out, a triumphant grin on my face as I escaped his grasp. But, just as I thought I was free, he surprised me by embracing me from behind, his arms enveloping me in a possessive hold.

In a sudden frenzy of panic, I began screaming and striking at his hand, causing confusion to flicker across his face. He seemed perplexed by my sudden outburst, considering the apparent compliance I had shown moments before. However, before he could comprehend my change in demeanor, the atmosphere shifted dramatically as a group of people burst into the house.

Among them were police officers and reporters, their presence signaling the abrupt end to his scheme. As the head of the police force stepped forward and declared his arrest, the gravity of the situation settled heavily upon him.

Meanwhile, my friend and a team of bodyguards rushed in to ensure my safety, their concern evident as they checked on my well-being. As the police began to escort him away, I gave him a subtle wink.

At that moment, realization dawned upon him like a storm, his anger boiling beneath the surface as he understood the depth of my deception. Yet, as he was dragged away by the authorities, he was powerless to retaliate, forced to face the consequences of his actions.

The next day, the news of Amod Agni, the son of a rich and infamous family being arrested by the police red-handed spread like wildfire. His family tried everything in their power to bring him out, but, they couldn't do anything.

CHAPTER XI

Swastika

Swastika's Parent's Home

Tension was high as I stood in front of my whole family. My grandfather, the patriarch of the family, sat on the large sofa with a stern expression on his face. To his right, my father sat, his face etched with concern. On the two single-sitting sofas on either side, my mother and brother watched the scene unfold, their expressions a mix of curiosity and apprehension.

My grandfather's anger radiated throughout the room, directed at me for daring to take such a risk and going against the powerful Agni family. He scolded me fiercely, his voice booming with authority. I tried to defend my actions, providing explanations and reasoning, but it seemed like an uphill battle. Some of my family members occasionally supported my grandfather's point of view, while others offered subtle gestures of support toward me.

As the heated discussion continued for what felt like an eternity, I could feel the weight of their disappointment and concern. I knew they only wanted to protect me, but I also had to stand up for what was right.

Finally, my father spoke up, his voice calm yet filled with determination. "I understand your concerns, Father, but we cannot simply ignore the injustice happening around us. Our family has always stood for justice and righteousness. We cannot turn a blind eye to the actions of the Agni family."

My mother nodded in agreement, her eyes filled with unwavering support. "Our child has shown great courage and resilience. We should be proud of her for standing up for what is right."

My grandfather's stern expression softened, and he looked at me with a mixture of pride and concern. "You have always been headstrong, my child. While I worry for your safety, I cannot deny that your actions display the strength of our family's spirit."

A sense of relief washed over me as my family's support became evident. It was a reminder that even in the midst of disagreements, love and unity prevailed. We may have different opinions, but at the core, we were bound by a shared sense of justice and the unbreakable ties of family.

From that day onwards, I knew that my family, despite their reservations, would stand by my side. Their unwavering support would provide the strength and courage I needed to face the challenges that lay ahead.

A few days passed by in peace. A sense of false security settled over us, as we believed that the Agni family had retreated. Little did we know, they were just biding their time, waiting for the perfect moment to strike.

One day, while I was returning from the office. A van stopped beside me, and a group of people with black masks popped out. They sprayed chloroform at me, and I lost consciousness. By the time I woke up, I was in an abandoned factory, tied up.

Suddenly, I heard some footsteps coming. "Hi, Baby! Long time no see."

I instantly recognized that voice. It was Amod. I was confused for a bit and also scared. Amod was supposed to be in jail. How could he be there?

I protested. I shouted and tried to break free, but the ropes wouldn't loosen up.

"You bastard, leave me. How the hell did you come out of jail?"

"There is nowhere my family's influence can't reach, baby."

He slowly moved in my direction. Suddenly, the air seemed to be changing. He tugged my hair, forcing me to look up. His expression changed, and he could no longer smile. He slapped me hard. I felt a strong sensation, and my cheeks turned warm with pain and anger. And then, he slapped me again.

"You bastard! I will send you back to jail."

After listening to my remarks. He lost control and kicked me multiple times. I vomited blood. When I looked like I was about to die, his subordinates stopped him.

I lost consciousness.

By the time I woke up, there was no one else in the room. I couldn't even speak or ask for help.

As I was held captive, fear and despair consumed me. It was then that I discovered the depths of their corruption. His subordinates were talking about it on the other side of the room. Amod's family, using their ill-gotten power and influence, bribed officers to grant temporary release to the vile bastard who had tormented me. He was set free for just an hour, enough time for him to unleash his sadistic torment upon me.

The agony I endured at his hands was unbearable, both physically and mentally. His actions were ruthless, leaving me scarred and broken. Once he was satisfied with his wicked deed, he returned to the confines of prison, leaving behind a trail of darkness and deceit. To cover their tracks, they tampered with the CCTV footage, erasing any evidence of his temporary release.

Alone and shattered, I struggled to find solace and justice. The trauma I experienced haunted me, and the knowledge that the Agni family could continue their wicked ways unchecked weighed heavily on my soul. No one knew of their vile plot, and the walls of silence closed in around me.

I was rescued three days later. My family found out my whereabouts and came to rescue me. My brother and our bodyguards crashed all the goons. All I could see was my brother before I lost consciousness again.

*

I slowly opened my eyes. The room was too bright, so I covered my eyes with my hand. I found myself lying in a sterile hospital room. The faint beeping of machines served as a reminder of the ordeal I had just endured.

My brother, Arjun, sat by my side, his face etched with concern and relief. "Swastika, thank the heavens you're awake! We were so worried about you."

"Arjun, what happened? How did you find me?"

Arjun squeezed my hand reassuringly. We received a tip about your whereabouts. Our bodyguards swiftly mobilized and raided the location where you were being held captive.

I was so overwhelmed that my eyes became watery. "I can't believe you saved me. Thank you, Arjun. I don't know what I would have done without you."

"Stupid girl." He hit my head gently. "You're my sister. Protecting you is my duty. I would do anything to keep you safe."

"I'm so grateful to have you as my brother. I thought I was all alone in this nightmare."

"You're never alone, Swastika. We're a family, and we stick together no matter what. Now, focus on your recovery. You've been through so much, but we'll make sure you get back on your feet."

I nodded with determination. "I won't let this break me. I will find the strength to move forward and bring those responsible to justice."

Arjun placed a hand on my shoulder. "I believe in you. We'll do whatever it takes to ensure they pay for what they've done."

As our conversation subsided, a sense of gratitude and determination filled the room. I knew that with my brother by my side, I would find the strength to overcome the trauma I had endured. Together, we would face the challenges ahead and bring an end to the darkness that had tainted our lives.

After I finished narrating my story, I looked at Tarun. "Two months later, Anirudh entered the picture. And, you're familiar with what happened afterward, right?"

Tarun nodded.

CHAPTER XII

Swastika

Swastika's Parent's Home

Since that incident, Amod just won't leave me alone. So, my grandfather even considered sending me away.

My brother Arjun, our parents, and I sat around the coffee table, each lost in our own thoughts. Meanwhile, our grandfather stood by the fireplace, his gaze fixed on the dancing flames.

After a few minutes of silence, I finally said, "Father, I understand your concerns, but sending me away to B City won't solve anything. We need to find a way to bring justice to those responsible for what happened. It's not just about me, but also about all those girls who are victims of Amod's heinous deeds." My voice carried the weight of the collective suffering endured by his victims.

He sighed. "Swastika, my dear, I've been looking into the situation. The Agni family has covered their tracks so well that it's going to be nearly impossible to bring them to justice. They have powerful connections and are well-versed in manipulating the system."

Arjun asked, "What did the investigation reveal? Have we made any progress?"

My father replied grimly, "I'm afraid the results are disheartening. The Agni family has managed to tamper with the CCTV footage, making it nearly impossible to prove their involvement. They have a network of influential individuals protecting them, and any attempts to expose them have been met with threats and intimidation."

I was enraged. “So, they’re getting away with everything? That’s not fair!”

My mother worriedly said, “Swastika, dear, we need to prioritize your safety. It’s not worth putting yourself at risk if we can’t guarantee justice.”

“I… I understand, Mother. But, it feels like giving up.”

My grandfather firmly said, “Swastika, it’s not giving up. It’s strategizing and ensuring that you remain safe while we work on finding another way to bring them to justice. Going to B City will give us time to gather more evidence, build a stronger case, and outsmart them.”

“I trust you, Grandfather. If you believe this is the best course of action, then I’ll go to B City. But, promise me, you won’t stop fighting for justice.”

Grandfather placed a comforting hand on my shoulder. “I promise, my dear. We won’t rest until those who have hurt you and others face the consequences of their actions. We’ll find another way, a way that will ensure justice is served.”

So, my grandfather talked to his friend and arranged a job for me in this company. The CEO is his son and also my father’s good friend. So, they don’t need to worry about my safety. They still assigned some of our bodyguards to accompany me, just to be cautious.

*

Tarun

“Swastika, I want you to know that I’ll always be here for you. You don’t have to face this alone.”

“Thank you, Tarun. I don’t know what I would do without you.”

Without hesitation, I pulled her into a warm embrace. I held her tightly, offering her comfort and support. Although I didn’t know if it was effective.

"You're not alone, Swastika. We'll get through this together." I reassured her.

"I trust you, Tarun. Your friendship means the world to me."

From that day, I checked in on her regularly, sending her funny texts to brighten her day.

I sent a text, "Just wanted to remind you that you're strong and amazing! Don't forget it!"

*

Swastika

I smiled as I received Tarun's message. His support and humor helped lift my spirits.

I replied, "Thanks, Tarun. Your messages always brighten my day!"

After that day, I trusted him more and more. With him by my side, I felt a sense of strength and reassurance, ready to face whatever challenges life threw our way. What was this feeling? I felt so peaceful and happy. With Tarun by my side, I guessed I would be able to feel this sense of assurance for a long time. Oh my god, what was this? Like or love? I didn't know. I didn't want to name it yet. Did he feel the same way? I didn't know.

I was in a daze, busy thinking all these things when a notification sound brought me back to reality. It was Tarun again. He had invited me to go to the beach to watch the sunset. I agreed happily.

*

CHAPTER XIII

Tarun

Sunset Beach

The golden hues of the setting sun cast a warm glow over the beach, creating an enchanting ambiance for Swastika and me as we sat side by side, our toes buried in the soft sand. The rhythmic sound of crashing waves filled the air, adding to the magic of the moment.

As my heart pounded in my chest, I took a deep breath and gathered the courage to confess my feelings to Swastika. I'd known for a while that I was in love with her, but I had tried to ignore these emotions, fearing that they might jeopardize our cherished friendship. But, as time went on, I realized that I couldn't keep my feelings bottled up any longer.

Looking into Swastika's eyes, I saw a reflection of the deep connection we shared, and I knew that this moment was both terrifying and exhilarating.

"Swastika, I have something I want to tell you."

Swastika turned to me, her eyes filled with curiosity and warmth, unknowingly melting my heart even further.

"What is it, Tarun?" she said softly.

I took a deep breath. "I love you. It might sound sudden, but I can't help the way I feel. You're incredible, Swastika, in every way possible. You're smart, beautiful, and kind, and I can't imagine my life without you."

As I spoke, baring my soul to Swastika, my voice trembled with vulnerability. I felt a mixture of fear and hope, knowing that this confession could change everything between us.

Swastika's eyes widened in surprise, her gaze locked with mine. I wondered what emotions were swirling inside her like a tempestuous sea. She might have never expected me to express my feelings so boldly. I hoped the sincerity in my words touched her.

I continued, "I know we've been friends for a while, and I cherish that. I don't want to risk losing what we have. But, I can't deny my feelings any longer. I want to be more than friends. I want to be your partner in life, to stand by your side and make you happy every day. So, Swastika, will you do me the honor of being my life partner?"

The air around us seemed to hold its breath as Swastika took in my heartfelt confession. The crashing waves provided a soothing soundtrack, as if nature itself was awaiting her answer.

Swastika's mind raced, her heart torn between the joy of hearing my feelings and the fear of what it might mean for our friendship. Yet, as she looked into my eyes, she saw a vulnerability and sincerity that she had never seen before. She knew that she couldn't ignore her own feelings any longer either.

She grinned widely. "Tarun, I never expected this, but I'm so glad you said it. You mean the world to me, and I can't imagine a life without you either."

A sense of relief washed over me as I heard Swastika's response. I couldn't help but feel overjoyed that she didn't reject my feelings, and the weight of my confession started to lift.

"Yes, Hero. I would love to be your life partner."

My heart skipped a beat at her words, and I felt a surge of happiness I had never experienced before. With a beaming smile, I pulled Swastika into a tender embrace, feeling a sense of fulfillment and contentment like never before.

As we watched the sunset together, wrapped in each other's arms, I knew that this moment marked the beginning of a new chapter in our lives — one filled with love, trust, and the promise of a beautiful future together. The sun dipped below the horizon, leaving behind a sky painted with hues of pink and orange, mirroring the vibrant emotions that swirled within our hearts.

*

Swastika

My heart was still soaring with happiness from the beautiful confession I just shared with Tarun. The smile on my face was radiant as I stood in front of the mirror, basking in the afterglow of our special moment.

My mobile buzzed. As I picked up the phone and heard my brother's voice, curiosity bubbled up inside me.

"Swastika, I have some news for you," he said, his tone serious.

My excitement dimmed slightly as I listened intently.

"Oh, hey! What's up?" I replied, trying to maintain my cheerful demeanor. "Guess what? I have some amazing news to share with you!" I added, hoping to lighten the mood.

But, my brother's next words sent a chill down my spine. "I'm glad you're happy, but there's something important you need to know," he said solemnly.

My heart skipped a beat as I braced myself for what was to come.

"We have finally gathered enough evidence against the Agni family, and we have to go to court in M City," he continued, his voice heavy with significance.

The weight of his words sank in, and a sense of dread washed over me.

Court? So soon? I thought to myself, struggling to process the news. Despite my efforts to keep my composure, a wave of conflicting emotions threatened to overwhelm me.

"Yes, it's happening sooner than we expected," my brother said sympathetically, sensing my unease. "We need to be there to ensure that justice is served."

His words offered little comfort as I grappled with the uncertainty of what lay ahead.

A whirlwind of emotions flooded my mind. Relief washed over me at the thought of finally holding the Agni family accountable for their actions. But, alongside that relief, a pang of sadness tugged at my heartstrings. Leaving Tarun behind, especially now that our relationship had just begun, felt like tearing away a piece of myself.

"I... I don't know how to feel about this," I admitted, my voice tinged with sadness. "I'm happy that justice will be served, but I'm also sad to leave Tarun behind and go back to M City. We just started dating."

"I know it's not easy, Swastika," he said gently. "But, we have to do this. We have to make sure that they pay for what they did to you and other girls."

His words resonated with me, stirring a sense of determination within me. Despite the tears welling up in my eyes, I nodded in agreement.

"You're right," I said, my voice filled with resolve. "We can't let them get away with what they did. I'll go back to M City and face whatever comes our way."

"That's the spirit, sis," he said proudly. "We'll face this together, just like we always have."

At that moment, I found strength in his support, knowing that no matter what lay ahead, we'd navigate it together.

I took a deep breath. I knew that I had to be strong, not just for myself, but for my family and for Tarun as well. With tears glistening in my eyes, I offered a grateful smile to my brother.

"Thank you for being there for me, always," I said, my voice soft but sincere.

His warm response filled me with comfort. "You don't have to thank me, Swastika," he assured me. "We're family, and I'll always be here for you. Now, let's prepare for the journey ahead. We'll face whatever comes our way together."

"Tarun and I started dating." As soon as I said this, the weight of the serious matter lifted.

My brother's teasing lightened the mood further. "Aha... my dear sis has fallen in love. When did this happen, sis?"

I chuckled in response, feeling a mixture of embarrassment and amusement. "Hey, hey... stop teasing me," I retorted, trying to brush off his playful banter. "We started dating today."

After exchanging a few more lighthearted remarks, I reluctantly ended the call. The impending court proceedings weighed heavily on my mind, but I took solace in my brother's support and Tarun's love.

As thoughts of Tarun filled my mind, a sense of sadness washed over me, tempered by a glimmer of hope. Despite the distance that would soon separate us, I clung to the belief that our love would endure. With a deep breath, I steeled myself for the challenges ahead, determined to face them with courage and resilience.

CHAPTER XIV

Swastika

Swastika's Home

Sitting on the couch, I felt the familiar weight of my phone in my hands, my heart pounding with nervous anticipation. I had to tell Tarun about my upcoming trip to M City for the court proceedings, but the thought filled me with uncertainty.

Summoning my courage, I dialed Tarun's number, each ring echoing loudly in my ears as I waited anxiously for him to pick up. When he finally answered, his voice was filled with excitement, and I couldn't help but smile despite my apprehension.

"Hey, Swastika! I was just about to call you," Tarun said, his enthusiasm evident in his tone. "I couldn't stop thinking about today."

Struggling to match his excitement, I replied, "Hi, Tarun. Yeah, it was a beautiful moment, wasn't it?"

My attempt to hide my unease fell flat, and Tarun picked up on the subtle shift in my tone.

"Is everything okay, Swastika?" he asked, his concern palpable even through the phone line. "You sound a bit down."

As I mustered the courage to share the news with Tarun, my heart felt heavy with the weight of the impending separation. His surprised reaction only amplified my own feelings of sadness.

"Well, there's something I need to tell you," I began, the words catching in my throat. "My brother just called, and they have gathered enough evidence. We have to go to court in M City."

"Oh... that is great," he said surprised. I could sense Tarun's disappointment as he processed the news, his voice tinged with concern. "When do you have to leave?"

With a touch of sadness, I replied, "In a few days. I'll be away for a while."

The thought of being apart from Tarun gnawed at me, but I knew it was necessary to seek justice for what happened.

Tarun's determination took me by surprise as he declared, "I will come along, Swastika. I want to be there with you."

His unwavering support filled me with warmth, but I couldn't help feeling shocked by his sudden offer.

"What? But, Tarun, you don't have to come," I protested, my voice tinged with concern. "It's going to be dangerous, and I don't want to put you at risk."

Tarun's firm response cut through my objections. "I don't care about the risk. I care about you. I want to support you and be by your side through this. We're in this together, remember?"

Hearing Tarun's words, I was deeply touched by the sincerity and depth of his feelings for me. His offer to accompany me to M City caught me off guard, and I was momentarily at a loss for words.

"Tarun, I... I don't know what to say," I managed to whisper, my emotions swirling as I tried to process his unexpected kindness.

Tarun's voice was earnest, filled with determination. "Just say you want me to come with you. I promise I'll be there for you, whatever the situation is."

As I listened to him, my heart swelled with love and gratitude. I never imagined he would want to come with me, to stand by my side during such a difficult time. The thought of facing this challenge with him filled me with a newfound hope and happiness.

A smile spread across my face as I responded, "Tarun, I would be so happy if you came with me. Thank you for offering to support me through this."

His smile mirrored my own, warm and reassuring. "It's my pleasure, Swastika. We're a team, remember? Together, we can face anything."

Tears welled up in my eyes as I realized how lucky I was to have someone like him in my life.

"Yes, together," I said, my voice thick with emotion. "I'm so grateful to have you in my life."

Tarun's voice softened as he spoke tenderly, "And, I'm grateful to have you in mine. We'll get through this, Swastika, I promise."

As we shared this tender moment over the phone, I felt a deep sense of love and connection with Tarun. It was like our hearts were intertwined. I knew the journey ahead wouldn't be easy — there were so many challenges and uncertainties waiting for us. But, at that moment, all I could think about was how grateful I was to have him in my life.

With Tarun by my side, I felt stronger and more hopeful than ever before. No matter what came our way, I knew we could lean on each other and support one another through it all. That thought filled me with a warmth and comfort I'd never felt before.

The next morning, I accompanied Tarun to his parents' house to discuss our relationship. As we entered the living room, I could sense the surprise in their expressions. It was evident that seeing Tarun with a girl was unexpected for them, considering his reserved personality.

"Mom, Dad, this is Swastika," Tarun began, his voice slightly nervous. "She is my girlfriend. I would like to ask you for your approval of our relationship."

Their initial surprise quickly turned into shock as they exchanged bewildered glances. It took them a moment to process what Tarun had just said.

"Is it really true that you both are in a relationship? I can't believe it," his mother exclaimed, her disbelief evident in her voice.

"Honey, pinch my hand," his father joked, prompting a playful reaction from his wife.

"Ah! So, it is real. I am not dreaming," he responded, finally coming to terms with the situation.

I couldn't help but chuckle nervously at their reactions, though I tried to maintain my composure. Despite my nerves, the lighthearted banter between Tarun's parents made the atmosphere more relaxed.

"Oh, my dear Swastika, how did you fall for this boring son of mine?" Tarun's mother teased, earning a mock offended look from her husband.

"He is as boring as his father," she continued, eliciting laughter from all of us.

"Ahem! Ahem! Honey, you are defaming me and our son in front of our soon-to-be daughter-in-law," Tarun's father interjected with a playful tone.

"It is the truth anyway!" she retorted, maintaining her stance.

Their playful bickering brought a smile to my face, and I couldn't help but imagine Tarun and I growing old together, sharing similar moments of lighthearted banter.

Amidst the laughter, Tarun's father finally spoke up, shifting the conversation to a more serious note. "Jokes apart, let's talk business now."

I braced myself for a more formal discussion, ready to address any concerns they might have about our relationship. After all, Tarun's father, being a government official in a high position, likely had certain expectations for his son's future.

Tarun's father cleared his throat, signaling the transition to a more serious discussion. "While humor has its place, let's address the matter at hand. Swastika, Tarun, I must admit this news comes as a surprise to us. However, we respect your decision and are willing to listen."

I nodded, grateful for his openness to discuss the matter further. "Thank you, Sir," I replied respectfully. "I understand that our relationship might not fit the expectations you had, but I assure you, Tarun and I are committed to each other and our future."

Tarun's father nodded thoughtfully, his expression serious yet contemplative. "Swastika, Tarun, I won't deny that our family comes from a different background than yours. We may not have the same wealth or status, but we value integrity, hard work, and family above all else."

He paused, his gaze shifting between Tarun and me. "I have concerns about how you both will navigate the challenges that come with such differences. However, I also believe that love transcends such barriers if nurtured with understanding and respect."

Tarun spoke up, his voice filled with determination. "Dad, I understand your concerns, but Swastika and I are willing to face those challenges together. We've already discussed our goals and aspirations, and we're committed to supporting each other every step of the way."

Tarun's father nodded with a hint of pride in his eyes. "Very well, then. If you both are truly committed to making this work, I won't stand in your way. However, I do have one condition."

We both looked at him, eager to hear his condition.

"I want to see you both thrive together, not just in your personal relationship, but also in your careers. Swastika, I know you come from a successful family, but I want to see you stand on your own feet, independent of your family's wealth."

I nodded, understanding his point. "I agree, Sir. I've always believed in the importance of earning my own success, and I'm determined to do so."

His mother intervened and said, "And don't forget about kids. I want you to have at least two kids," earning a glare from her husband.

"What? Growing the family tree is just as important," she retorted.

I responded, "Don't worry about that, Mam. I like kids as well."

He turned to Tarun. "As for you, Tarun, I expect you to support Swastika in her endeavors, just as she will support you. And, I want to see you both working towards a shared future with dedication and sincerity."

Tarun nodded firmly. "I understand, Dad. I'll do everything in my power to make sure Swastika and I have a bright future together."

With that, Tarun's father extended his hand towards me. "Welcome to the family, Swastika."

I shook his hand, feeling a sense of relief wash over me. Despite the initial surprise and uncertainty, Tarun's family had accepted our relationship with open arms, and I couldn't be happier. We had their blessing to move forward together, and I was eager to embark on this journey with Tarun by my side.

CHAPTER XV

Arjun

M City Airport

I stood anxiously at the airport, waiting for my sister, Swastika, to arrive. It had been a while since we had seen each other, and I couldn't wait to see her again. As I scanned the crowd, I spotted her walking towards me, and I couldn't help but smile at the sight of her.

"Swastika! Over here!" I called out excitedly.

"Arjun! It's so good to see you!" she responded, grinning from ear to ear.

We hugged tightly, and I felt a rush of emotions. It was great to have her back, especially after everything she had been through. But, as I pulled away from the hug, I noticed someone standing next to her, and my eyes widened in surprise.

"And, who is this handsome gentleman?" I asked teasingly.

Swastika blushed, shooting a playful glare in my direction. "Arjun, this is Tarun. He's a colleague and my boyfriend. Tarun, meet my brother, Arjun."

"Nice to meet you, Arjun," Tarun said, extending his hand. "Swastika has told me so much about you."

"Likewise, Tarun," I replied, shaking his hand. "Nice to meet you too."

As we walked out of the airport, I could see the easy camaraderie between Swastika and Tarun. They seemed comfortable and happy in each other's company, and it made me feel at ease knowing that my sister had someone like Tarun by her side.

"So Tarun, you better take good care of my sister, alright?" I teased, glancing between the two of them.

Tarun smiled warmly and responded, "I promise, Arjun. She's in good hands."

Swastika playfully chimed in, "I can take care of myself, you know!"

I laughed, shaking my head. "Of course you can, sis. But, it's always nice to have someone looking out for you."

Swastika's expression softened, and she nodded, her voice quieter. "Yeah, it is."

As we continued to joke and laugh, I felt a sense of relief knowing that Swastika had someone like Tarun in her life. He seemed like a genuine and caring person, and I couldn't help but feel grateful to him for bringing a smile back to my sister's face. As we headed out of the airport together, I knew that this trip was going to be filled with laughter, love, and fun, thanks to Tarun's presence in our lives.

*

Tarun

I sat in the backseat of the car while Swastika sat in the front. Arjun was driving, occasionally glancing at her with a warm smile.

"So, how was the flight?" he asked, smiling.

"It was good," Swastika replied, grinning. "But, you know what made it even better? Having Tarun by my side."

"Oh, I can see that. You two were practically glued to each other the whole time," Arjun teased, making Swastika blush.

"Arjun, stop teasing me!" she said, laughing.

"I'm just glad to see you happy, sis," Arjun responded with a chuckle.

As we reached the hotel, Swastika's excitement grew. She couldn't wait to show me the beautiful suite they had booked for us.

"I hope you like the hotel, Tarun. I wanted to make sure you're comfortable during your stay here," she said excitedly.

"I'm sure he'll love it. You've thought of everything, as always," Arjun added, smiling.

We went to the reception to check in.

"Good afternoon. How may I assist you?" the receptionist asked with a smile.

"Hi, we have a reservation for Tarun," Swastika grinned.

The receptionist checked the computer. "Ah, yes. Mr. Tarun. We have a beautiful suite reserved for you."

"Thank you so much," I said, grateful.

"You're going to love it, Tarun. It's a big suite with a stunning view of the city," Swastika said excitedly.

"I'm looking forward to it," I replied, smiling.

After checking in, we made our way to the suite. Swastika's heart swelled with happiness as she saw the awe in my eyes at the sight of the luxurious room.

"Wow, this is incredible," I said, amazed.

"I'm glad you like it," Swastika grinned.

"Thank you, Swastika. You really didn't have to do all this for me."

"I wanted to, Tarun," she replied softly. "You mean a lot to me, and I want you to have a great stay in M City."

"You're too kind, Swastika. I can't thank you enough."

As Swastika and Arjun left the hotel to head home, Swastika couldn't stop smiling.

*

Swastika

Swastika's Parent's Home

As we entered the familiar living room, I couldn't help but feel a sense of warmth and comfort wash over me. My family surrounded me with hugs and smiles, and I felt a wave of love and happiness in their presence.

"It's so good to be back home!" I exclaimed, grinning widely.

My mother, with tears in her eyes, rushed forward, wrapping me in a warm embrace.

"Oh, my dear Swastika, we missed you so much!" she said, her voice filled with emotion.

My father looked at me with pride, his eyes softening as he said, "You look more beautiful than ever, my daughter."

I blushed slightly.

Arjun, always the teaser, chimed in, "I hope you didn't miss us too much with your new friend around."

I playfully nudged him, saying, "Oh, don't worry, Arjun. You know you're irreplaceable."

Arjun smirked, responding, "Damn right, I am."

Laughter filled the room, and I felt a deep sense of gratitude for the love and support of my family.

CHAPTER XVI

Swastika

Courtroom

The courtroom was filled with tension and anticipation as we waited for our turn to present our case.

The lawyer leaned in and whispered, "Don't worry. We have a strong case, and the evidence you've provided is solid. We'll make sure justice is served."

Feeling nervous, I replied, "Thank you. I just hope everything goes smoothly."

Tarun placed a supportive hand on my shoulder and reassured me, "We're all here for you, Swastika. We'll get through this together."

Arjun, with firm resolve, added, "And we won't back down until those responsible are held accountable."As our turn came, I took a deep breath and stepped up to the stand.

The Chief Ministerial Officer, Sherestedar, calmly instructed, "Please proceed."

I, now more confident, began, "Your Honor, we have evidence that proves that Amod and his family have been involved in heinous crimes. They have manipulated, threatened, and harmed innocent people to cover up their tracks. We have witness testimonies, documents, and surveillance footage that support our claims."

The lawyer submitted the necessary documents.

As they left the courtroom, I felt a mix of emotions. I was relieved to have finally filed the case, but the weight of the situation still hung heavily on my shoulders.

Tarun placed a comforting hand on my shoulder and said, "You did great, Swastika. We'll get through this together."

I smiled weakly. "Thank you, Tarun. I just hope justice is served."

Arjun, with determination in his voice, added, "We won't stop until it is. We'll fight for the truth and for all those who have suffered because of them."

"I'm lucky to have both of you by my side."

We walked out of the courthouse, ready to face whatever challenges lay ahead. We knew that the road to justice wouldn't be easy, but we were determined to see it through.

*

A Few Days Later

The courtroom was filled with tension as Amod stood on one side, and we on the other.

Tarun whispered, "Stay strong, Swastika. We know the truth, and we have the evidence to prove it."

"I hope justice prevails, Tarun."

As the hearing began, the Agni family tried their best to manipulate the situation. They presented false claims and fabricated evidence, attempting to turn the blame on me and paint me as the instigator.

Their lawyer, Mr Kapoor, said, "Your Honor, Miss Swastika has approached my client in the first place with ill intention. Please check these messages she sent to my client, Amod. You can see how explicit they are. My client only tried to make a move on her because she was the one who seduced him first."

I couldn't help but clench my fists, my knuckles turning white, as I watched the altered messages being displayed on the screen. I knew that these messages were far from the truth, but the Agni family was trying everything they could to tarnish my reputation.

As Mr Kapoor continued to make baseless claims, I felt a burning rage building within me. I couldn't believe how could they make such claims. I tried to remain composed. I knew very well that we could counter these false claims with our own evidence. Tarun squeezed my hand to reassure me.

Our lawyer, Mr Babu quickly countered the false claims with the truth, presenting the real evidence that proved Amod's wicked deeds.

"Your Honor, social media chats can be manipulated. These are the original chats and these documents prove their authenticity, provided by the forensic experts."

Mr Babu passed those documents to the judge. I calmed down a little seeing the truth coming out one by one. Fortunately, we came prepared.

Mr Kapoor's face was pale now, but he did not back down yet. He brought up the topic of Swastika being kidnapped by Amod.

"Your Honor, how will they justify their false claims that Amod kidnapped Swastika? When my client was in the police station at that time."

Now, it was our time to counter. They must have thought that we had no evidence. Two days ago, we had provoked the officer who helped the Agni family to spill the beans.

We went to the station and Arjun said, "Officer, you do know that you have committed a crime, right? We will put you behind bars in two days."

"Oh really? How? Where is the evidence?"

"CCTV footage," I said from behind.

He started laughing. "There is no such footage."

"How so, Officer? At least there should be footage that Amod was in jail."

"I deleted everything. Now what can you do? Now, get out of here. Otherwise, I will book a nuisance case on all of you for coming to the station and spouting nonsense."

We all stepped out of the station since we got the evidence we wanted in our spy camera.

*

Lawyer Mr Babu

Tarun gave me a pen drive earlier, and I presented the video evidence to the judge.

Upon seeing what the officer was saying in the video, the Agni family's faces went pale. But, they quickly recovered. They must have come prepared for this. As expected, that officer wouldn't have sat still after that conversation with Tarun and Arjun.

"Your Honor, there is no such thing as deleting footage. A 24-hour footage is present for the date 9th April 2023."

"Lawyer Kapoor, how do you know which day's footage we are talking about? I never mentioned any date. Please make a note, Your Honor."

I didn't stop there. I also asked the judge to see the other footage videos in the pen drive. Those were the footage of Amod going out of the police station and the shops on the route Amod traveled on that day. It looked like they tried to avoid traffic cameras but forgot about the possibility of shops having CCTVs. Tarun and Arjun managed to persuade the shop owners to give us footage, but we couldn't see Amod's face in two of those footage. We were worried that they would escape easily until last night.

Last night, Tarun hacked the database and retrieved the backup footage. I was against the idea at first since he might be punished for hacking the government database. But, he was willing to take the risk for Swastika. I, eventually, gave in. Tarun asked me to keep it a secret from her as she might not agree to this.

After seeing all the footage, the Agni family went speechless. Lawyer Kapoor couldn't even counter. Since they couldn't escape, they started blaming Tarun for hacking.

"Your Honor, evidence obtained by illegal means can't be taken into consideration."

"Your Honor, even though it is obtained by illegal means, one can't deny what is in the footage. The surveillance and software department of police can prove its authenticity."

The judge thought for a moment and said, "Although the evidence is obtained by illegal means, the court will take this into consideration understanding the seriousness of this case. Mr Rao is suspended and sentenced to one year of imprisonment for helping a criminal. And, Mr Tarun is given a warning to not do anything illegal, even if it is for helping people, and is fined Rs. 5000."

Then, I said, "Your Honor, not only that, my client Ms Swastika has gone through all this to bring justice to all the girls Amod has harassed in the past. We found out that there are many more victims than those who have come forward to provide their testimonies and evidence. Here are the testimony videos and related evidence. All of them were either bribed or threatened to keep quiet."

Old Mr Agni was furious that they didn't know what Swastika and the rest had been doing for the case without them having any idea.

The judge said, "This is a grave matter. We will examine all evidence and testimonies thoroughly."

As the trial progressed, the truth began to unfold. Witness testimonies revealed the heinous acts committed by Amod and the Agni family's involvement in the cover-up. The courtroom gasped in shock as the extent of their wickedness came to light.

"The court condemns such actions and will ensure that justice is served."

In the end, the truth prevailed, and Amod and the Agni family were held accountable for their wicked deeds. They were sentenced to jail, and their reign of terror came to an end.

CHAPTER XVII

Tarun

Courtroom

"Justice has been served, Swastika." I hugged her with happiness.

"I can't thank you enough, Tarun. You and Arjun stood by me throughout all of this."

"We're family, Swastika. We will always stand together, no matter what." Arjun smiled.

As we left the courtroom, a sense of closure and relief washed over us. The journey had been arduous, but justice had been served. I see that Swastika felt a weight lifted off her shoulders, knowing that she could finally move forward without the burden of Amod's wickedness hanging over her.

She looked at me. I couldn't understand what that look meant, but then she said, "With you and Arjun by my side, I knew that I could face anything that life threw my way."

Then she smiled as bright as a sun. This was the moment I fell for her again.

*

Swastika

Swastika's Parent's Home

I sat nervously at the dining table, my heart pounding in my chest. Beside me, Tarun held my hand reassuringly, giving me the strength to face my family.

My grandfather, with a stern expression, asked, "So, you two are in a relationship?"

Taking a deep breath, I responded, "Yes, Grandfather. Tarun and I are in love."

My father, clearly concerned, added, "But, Swastika, you know how dirty it can be to get involved with someone from a different background."

Defensively, I replied, "I understand your concern, Father, but Tarun and I love each other. We have known each other for a long time, and I trust him completely."

My mother, speaking softly, said, "Swastika, we just want what's best for you. We worry about how you will be taken care of in a family that may not have the same resources as we do."

I firmly answered, "Mother, I appreciate your concern, but finances should not be the deciding factor in our relationship. Tarun and I are capable of taking care of ourselves. We don't need to depend on anyone else."

Tarun, supporting me, added, "That's right. I may not come from a wealthy family, but I am determined to work hard and build a successful career. I promise to take care of Swastika and provide for our future."

My grandfather, still skeptical, questioned, "And, what about the money you borrowed from Swastika?"

Tarun felt embarrassed. If it weren't for the catfight with his father, this wouldn't have come up now.

He sincerely replied, "I will pay it back before our marriage. I want to stand on my own feet before we get married. Swastika has her own dreams; I may not be able to support her financially, but I fully support her ambitions and goals. We can be a team, helping each other achieve our goals."

"Grandfather, it is just a small amount. Besides, I have my own money too. I have worked hard to build my career, and I will continue to do so. Tarun and I are equal partners in this relationship, and we will support each other in every way."

My grandfather, contemplating for a moment, said, “I see your determination, both of you. But I have one condition. Tarun, I want you to come and work in our company. I have heard about your intelligence and skills, and I believe you can contribute greatly.”

Tarun gratefully replied, “Thank you, Grandfather. I would be honored to work in your company.”

Finally, my grandfather softened. “Alright then. If you two are so determined, I won’t stand in your way. But, promise me that you will always support and respect each other.”

“We promise.”

As the tension eased, a sense of relief washed over me. I knew that I had the support of my family and that they believed in our love. With their blessings, I felt more confident than ever about our future together.

My mother smiled warmly and said, “We just want you to be happy, Swastika.”

My father nodded in agreement, adding, “And, if Tarun makes you happy, then that’s all that matters.”

My grandfather, spoke softly, “Take care of each other. I trust you both to make the right decisions.”

Tarun and I shared a loving look, knowing that we had overcome the first hurdle in our journey together. We understood that our love was strong enough to face any challenges that came our way, and with the support of our family, we felt ready to take on the world.

The End

CHAPTER XVIII

Epilogue

Swatika

Swastika Home

"Swastika, have you seen my phone anywhere?"

"No, Tarun, I haven't."

"Let me call you, maybe we'll find it faster that way."

"Okay."

The phone rang, and I glanced at the caller ID. It was saved as My Index 0.

Index 0? What's that supposed to mean? I wondered silently.

"Tarun, what's with this 'Index 0'?" I asked curiously.

He smiled. "In programming, indexing starts at 0. So, 'Index 0' means you're my number one, my top priority."

His words took me by surprise. Feeling happy, I smiled and hugged him tightly.

www.ingramcontent.com/pod-product-compliance
Lightning Source LLC
LaVergne TN
LVHW041132150826
845673LV00007B/2288

* 9 7 9 8 8 9 5 8 8 2 3 7 5 *